This edition published by Parragon Books Ltd in 2016

Parragon Books Ltd
Chartist House
15–17 Trim Street
Bath BA1 1HA, UK
www.parragon.com

ISBN 978-1-4748-4697-4

Printed in China

Storybook
Collection

Bath • New York • Cologne • Melbourne • Delhi
Hong Kong • Shenzhen • Singapore

Contents

Pups Save the Party 9

Pups Save Ryder's Robot 33

Pups Save a Pool Day 57

Pups Save the Turbots 81

Pups and the Big Freeze 105

Pups Save the Parade 131

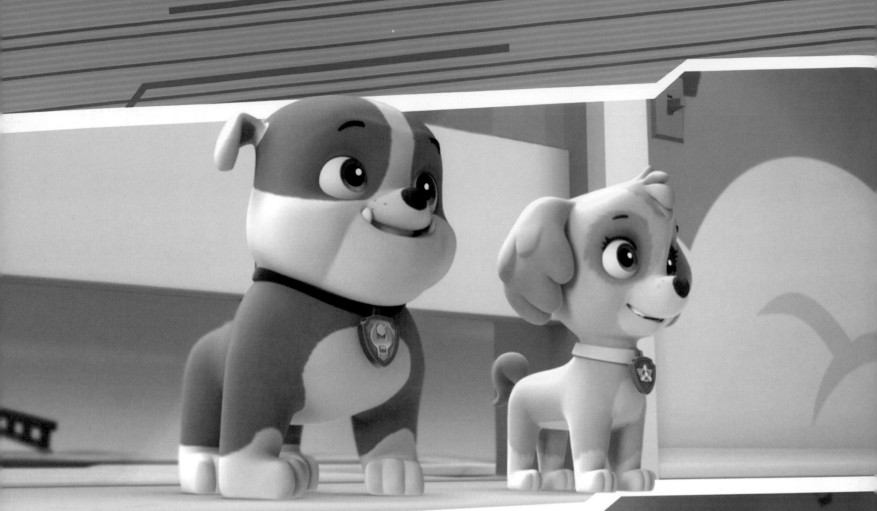

One windy afternoon, the pups are in Katie's Pet Parlour, preparing a surprise birthday party for Chase.

"Streamers away!" says Rocky.

"Next up – the birthday cake!" says Katie.

"But who is keeping Chase busy and making sure he doesn't find out about the party?" says Skye.

"Marshall is," says Rubble. "He can keep a secret ... can't he?"

Marshall and Chase are at the park.

"It's too windy," calls Chase. "Maybe we should go and find the others."

"No! I mean, uh ... it's nice here," says Marshall. "It's not like there's a big secret I have to keep...."

Suddenly, the wind gets so strong, it blows the pups onto the swings ... and they land in a heap on the floor.

Thump!

Back at the pet parlour, everyone is busy getting things ready for the party. Suddenly, the lights go off.

"All the lights are out on the street, too," calls Rocky. "What happened?"

Ryder looks at his PupPad. "If the power is out, something must be wrong with a windmill turbine on Jake's Mountain."

"We won't have any music without electricity!" cries Skye.

"Or lights," says Rubble. "Maybe we can't have a party for Chase after all."

"No way!" says Ryder. He grabs his PupPad.
"PAW Patrol to the Lookout!"

The pups all race to the tower, but there's
no electricity, so the lift isn't working.

"Marshall," says Ryder. "I need to use your ladder to get up to the Lookout."

Marshall raises his ladder and Ryder climbs up into the Lookout.

He looks through the periscope towards Jake's Mountain. "A windmill blade is broken," he says. "That's why there's no power."

"Pups, we have an emergency!" says Ryder.
"Rocky, I need you to find something in your
truck to fix that blade," he says.

"Marshall, we need your ladder to climb up
the windmill."

"Chase, the traffic lights will be out, too – we'll
need your siren and megaphone to direct traffic."

"And Skye, Rubble and Zuma," he whispers, "you look after the party." The pups nod back.

"Let's do this!" bark the PAW Patrol.

19

Skye, Rubble and Zuma stay behind at the Lookout.

"Time to save Chase's party!" says Skye.

"What are we going to do?" asks Zuma.

20

"We'll have a party in the dark," says Rubble.

"Yeah! We'll give Chase the best surprise party in the dark, ever!" barks Skye.

Over on Main Street, the traffic lights aren't working. There's a big traffic jam.

"We can't even cross the street," says Mayor Goodway. "And it's getting dark."

Chase arrives and gets straight to work with his megaphone.

"WOOF!" he barks. "Everyone going this way, go NOW! All the cars going that way, STOP!"

The drivers do as they're told and the traffic clears. The road is safe to cross.

Ryder, Marshall and Rocky are at the windmill.

"Let's get the electricity working for Chase's party," says Ryder, removing the broken blade.

"We can fix it with Zuma's old surfboard," says Rocky. "Why lose it when you can reuse it!"

Marshall raises his ladder. Rocky climbs up and attaches the surfboard to the windmill. Soon the wind picks up and it starts to turn.

"We did it!" shout Ryder, Marshall and Rocky.

Back at the pet parlour, the pups are playing in the dark when the lights come back on.

"Yes! Ryder and the PAW Patrol did it!" says Katie happily.

"But it's too late to bake a birthday cake," says Skye.

"I have an idea," says Katie.

On Main Street, the traffic lights come back on.

"Ryder and the PAW Patrol did it!" says Chase.
"All right, everyone, it's safe to cross."

"Thanks, Chase," say the people on Main Street.

Just then, Ryder calls on his helmet mic. "Change of plans, Chase. We need you at Katie's."

"On my way!" barks Chase.

Next, Ryder calls Skye. "Chase is on his way and so are we!" he tells her.

"The surprise is all ready," says Skye.

When Chase arrives at Katie's Pet Parlour, all the lights are off.

"Hello, anybody home?" he calls.

"SURPRISE!" everyone shouts, jumping out from behind the counter. "Happy Birthday, Chase!"

"You turned on the town's lights *and* made a party for me?" says Chase.

"Whenever it's your birthday, just yelp for help!" laughs Ryder.

31

"We couldn't make you a real cake, so I hope you like your dog-biscuit cake," says Katie.

"It's Chase's birthday," says Ryder, "but you've *all* been really good pups. Dig in!"

Chase blows out the candles and everyone cheers, then the pups eat cake. It's the best birthday ever!

Pups Save Ryder's Robot

Zing!

Ryder is switching on his new robot, Robo-dog, for the first time.

"OK, Robo-dog ... sit!" says Ryder.

"That's such a cool robot," says Skye.

"Thanks, I've just finished it," says Ryder. "Let's try digging!"

Ryder presses a button and Robo-dog tunnels underground at top speed.

Ryder peers down the hole. "Where did it go?" he says.

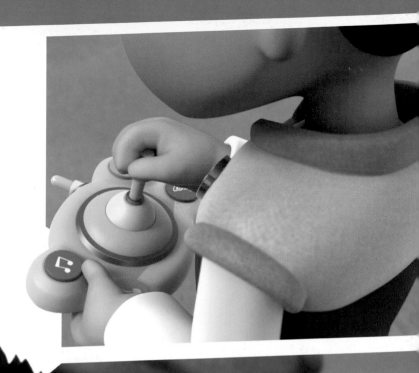

Zuma is asleep in his Pup House when Robo-dog pops up right underneath him.

"Whoa! Where did you come from?" says Zuma.

Ryder races around the corner. "Sorry, Zuma," he says. "I see you've met Robo-dog. Let's try ... flying instead!"

Robo-dog's paws turn into rockets and it floats up into the air.

"Wow!" everyone says.

"It should be able to run really fast, too," says Ryder.

Ready ...
set ...

"No robot can outrun me!" says Marshall. "Let's race."

Chase gets the pups into position, then uses his megaphone to shout, "Ready, set, GO!"

GO!

38

Marshall and Robo-dog start to race, but just as Marshall takes the lead, he trips and rolls into a log.

"I'm stuck!" he shouts.

"Hold on," says Ryder, pressing the robot's 'Turbo Power' button.

Robo-dog goes even faster, pushing Marshall out of the log with a *POP*! Then Robo-dog zooms on ahead.

Marshall tries to keep up, but stumbles into Ryder, who sits on Robo-dog!

Oof!

"Oh, no! The antenna is broken," says Marshall.

Robo-dog jumps up, twitching and buzzing. Ryder tries to stop it, but the robot digs a tunnel and disappears!

Suddenly, Robo-dog appears on Main Street.

It crashes straight into Mr Porter's fruit stall. Then it knocks Mayor Goodway off her feet, sending her flying into a flower display!

Mayor Goodway calls Ryder on her mobile phone. "Ryder, help! Someone's pet is on the loose!"

"That's my robot," says Ryder. "It's out of control, but we'll take care of it."

"PAW Patrol to the Lookout!" says Ryder.

The pups line up in the tower, ready for action.

"We have to stop Robo-dog before it causes any more trouble," says Ryder. "If we can turn it off, I can try and fix it."

"Skye, you should be able to spot it with your zoom goggles. And Rocky, I need you to help us build something so we can catch it."

"Let's take to the sky!" says Skye.

"Green means go!" barks Rocky.

"The rest of you, please tidy up the mess Robo-dog has made," says Ryder. "Let's roll!"

Pups away!

Skye is in the helicopter keeping track of Robo-dog.

"He's heading towards the water tower," says Skye.

Robo-dog crashes into the water tower and straight out of the other side. Then it flies through the pet parlour.

Katie and Cali jump out of the way ... and land in a bubble bath.

"Guess he didn't want to use the doggie door," says Katie.

Rubble and Zuma are on Main Street tidying up.

"Here's the last of the watermelons, Mr Porter," says Rubble.

"Thanks for helping, pups," says Mr Porter. "I think we got all of it."

But suddenly, Robo-dog appears and knocks them all over again.

Rubble sighs.

Skye calls Ryder on her helmet mic.

"Ryder! Your robot is in the air and it's heading straight for me!"

"Can you get him to fly towards Rocky's truck?" Ryder says.

"I'll do my best!" says Skye, looping away from the runaway robot.

Meanwhile, Rocky has been really busy making something to catch Robo-dog – a magnet launcher.

"Almost ready!" says Rocky.

Skye guides Robo-dog closer to Rocky and Ryder.

Rocky launches the magnet and it flies high into the air, then sticks to Robo-dog's metal body.

Whizz!

"Perfect shot, Rocky!" says Ryder. "You're on, Skye."

Skye lowers the helicopter's hook and catches the magnet. "Robo-dog is coming home!" she barks.

Skye lowers Robo-dog onto Mr Porter's patio.
It tries to run around but Ryder turns it off.

"I guess it's back to the drawing board with
this invention," says Ryder, sadly.

"Hold on, Ryder," says Rocky. "I've got an old antenna you can use."

Ryder changes the antenna and switches on Robo-dog.

The robot is back to normal. *BARK! BARK!*

"Thanks, Rocky! And thanks to all you pups, too,"
says Ryder. "I couldn't have fixed it without you!"

"Well, if you're ever in trouble, Ryder ..." says Rocky.

"Just yelp for help!" all the pups bark.

"What a good bunch of pups," says Ryder, smiling.

Pups Save
a Pool Day

It's a hot and sunny day in Adventure Bay.
Rocky and Rubble are in the park.

"I need to cool down," says Rubble.
"Let's take a dip in the pool!"

Rocky and Rubble head to the pool, but when they get there, it's empty!

"Oh, no! What happened to the water?" says Rocky.

"I don't know," says Rubble, "but we have to find out. This is a job for the PAW Patrol! Let's go."

Over at the Lookout, Skye and Marshall
are packing things for a day at the pool.

"Are you ready?" says Skye.

"Almost," calls Marshall.
"I just need my towel,
sun cream, hat, water and
my Super Dog comic book.
Now I'm ready!"

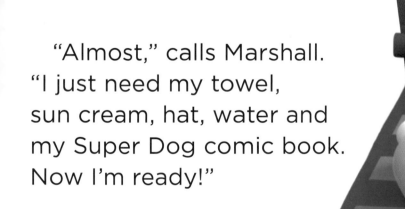

Rubble and Rocky race down Main Street, where they find Ryder and their friend Alex.

"Hey, pups," says Ryder. "What's wrong?"

"There's no water in the pool," pants Rocky.

"No water? What are we going to do?" asks Alex.

"Don't worry," says Ryder, pulling out his PupPad. "The PAW Patrol will fix it." He hits the alarm button and calls the pups to the Lookout.

The pups line up in the control room.

"The water from the water tower isn't reaching the pool," says Ryder. "We need to find out why."

"Marshall, I need your ladder to check out the tower. And Rubble, I need your shovel in case we need to dig up a blocked pipe."

The pups are excited to help.

"Everyone else, head to the pool!" says Ryder.

Ryder, Rubble and Marshall arrive at the water tower. The pad holding up the tower has slipped, and the water pipe is bent.

"We have to fix the tower before we can fix the pipe," says Ryder. "We just need a few more paws to help us!"

Ryder calls Rocky and Chase. "Chase, we need your winch. And Rocky, we need your forklift, too."

"You got it, Ryder!" bark Chase and Rocky.

When Rocky and Chase arrive at the
water tower, all the pups leap into action.

"Okay, PAW Patrol, you each have an
important job to do!" says Ryder.

"Chase, can we use your cable hook and winch motor?"

"On the way!" says Chase.

"Marshall," calls Ryder, "can you climb up and attach the hook to the tower?"

"Winch cable is hooked on!" says Marshall.

Next, Rubble uses his
digger to make a pile
of earth near the tower.

Let's dig it!

"Great job, Rubble," says Ryder. "Now Rocky, use your forklift to pick up the cement pad, so Rubble can put the earth underneath."

"Let's do it!" says Rocky.

Meanwhile at the pool, Skye has an idea to keep everyone cool. She flies right to the top of Jake's Mountain.

"What could be cooler than snow?" says Skye.

"Check it out," says Zuma. "Here's Skye to cool us off!"

But when Skye drops the snow, it all lands on Zuma!

"First I was a hot dog, now I'm an ice pup!" says Zuma.

Back at the water tower, the PAW Patrol
are finishing the repairs.

Chase pulls the tower with his winch.
Then Rocky lifts up the cement pad and
Rubble dumps earth under it.

"Cement pad, going back down," calls Rocky. When it's in place, Chase releases the winch. The water tower straightens out.

"Great!" says Ryder. "Now let's fix the bent pipe and get the water flowing again."

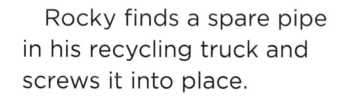

Rocky finds a spare pipe
in his recycling truck and
screws it into place.

"That should do it!"
says Rocky. "Let's see
if we fixed it."

76

Ryder calls Skye on the PupPad. "Skye, I'm just about to turn the water back on. The pool should start filling up any second now."

"Thanks, Ryder," says Skye. "Get ready, everyone, the water is on its way!"

Let's SWIM!

Everyone waits by the pool, then suddenly
a huge jet of water bursts out of the hose.
Their day at the pool is saved!

"Hooray!" they all cheer.

78

When the pool has filled up, Zuma says,
"All right, everybody. Ready, set ... get wet!"

Ryder and the other pups arrive at the pool.

"Thanks for fixing the pool, PAW Patrol!" says Alex.

"You're welcome, Alex," says Ryder. "And remember, whenever there's trouble, just yelp for help!"

Pups Save the Turbots

Ryder and the PAW Patrol are playing volleyball on the beach.

"Get the ball!" bark Zuma and Rubble.

The pups are soon joined by Captain Turbot and his friend.

"Hi, everyone," says Captain Turbot. "This is my cousin, François. He's from France."

"Ooh-la-la!" says François. "The only thing better than football is volleyball. Make room for one more!"

Captain Turbot leaves François to the volleyball game.

"I think I saw a blue-footed booby bird down by the bay," Captain Turbot tells Ryder. "If I can get a picture, it might make it onto the cover of *Marine-Bird Monthly*!"

"Good luck," calls Ryder.

Captain Turbot heads off in his boat. When he looks through his binoculars he sees François kitesurfing.

"I hope François' fancy footwork doesn't scare my bird away," Captain Turbot says to himself.

Wally the walrus pops up and barks loudly. At first Captain Turbot doesn't understand but when he looks at where Wally is pointing, he sees the blue-footed booby bird.

"Oh! There it is!" gasps Captain Turbot. "On my boat!"

Captain Turbot is so busy trying to take a photograph, he falls overboard and scares the booby bird.

"Oh, no! Come back!" cries Captain Turbot as the bird flies away.

Ryder and the pups are still playing
on the beach when Wally swims up.

"Hi, Wally," says Ryder. "What's wrong?"

Wally barks, points and flaps his flippers
until Ryder understands the problem.

88

"It's Captain Turbot!" says Ryder. "He found his bird, but lost his boat ... I think Wally is trying to tell us that the captain needs our help."

Ryder pulls out his PupPad. "No job is too big, no pup is too small. PAW Patrol to the Lookout!"

At the Lookout, the pups are ready for action.

"Pups, Captain Turbot needs us," says Ryder. "He was trying to take a photo of the blue-footed booby bird, but ended up in the bay."

"Zuma, I need you to use your lifebelt to rescue the captain and get him back to his boat."

"Let's dive in!" says Zuma.

"And Skye, I need you to search for the bird's nest from above."

"Let's take to the sky!" she says.

Ryder, Zuma and Skye
race across the bay.

"There he is!" cries Zuma.

"Hang on, Captain Turbot,"
calls Ryder. "Zuma will get
you – I'll rescue your boat."

Zuma launches the lifebelt. It lands over Captain Turbot and Zuma pulls him back to his hovercraft.

"Woo-hoo! Thanks, Zuma," says Captain Turbot.

Zuma and Captain Turbot climb aboard the Flounder. Ryder and Skye are already there waiting.

"We'll help you get some pictures of the booby bird," says Ryder.

"Thank you," says Captain Turbot.

Suddenly, François surfs in, almost knocking over his cousin.

"Okay, Horatio. I will take a picture of this bird for you."

Captain Turbot sighs.

Meanwhile, Skye is flying across the bay looking for the blue-footed booby bird. She spots its nest on the cliff top.

"That's it!" Skye shouts into her helmet mic. "I couldn't miss those bright blue feet!"

"Bingo!" cries Captain Turbot. "You've found it!"

To everyone's surprise, François takes off on his kitesurf board.

"Wait," says Captain Turbot. "You're going to scare the booby bird!"

But François calls back, "I will get the photo for you!"

François lands near the bird and gets out his camera.

"Say 'Le Cheese'!" shouts François. The booby bird flies straight at him.

"Mad booby bird!" cries François.

François falls off the cliff edge and clings on with one hand!

Skye quickly flies over. She lowers Captain Turbot down to François.

"Hang on, François," calls Captain Turbot. "Help is here!"

"Help, Horatio!" cries François. "This is a very angry bird."

The booby bird hops onto François' hand. He lets go of the cliff in fright and lands in the sea.

SPLASH!

The PAW Patrol help François onto the boat and Captain Turbot turns to the booby bird.

"Hello, beautiful birdie," says Captain Turbot. "Can I take your picture, please?"

The bird poses happily.

CLICK!

Later, on the boat, François is shivering.

"Are you okay?" says Captain Turbot.

"I am," says François. "Thanks to you, Horatio. And the PAW Patrol."

Later, at the park, Captain Turbot gives Ryder a present.

"I brought you this picture of the blue-footed booby bird to thank you," says Captain Turbot.

"Thanks!" says Ryder. "Whenever you're in trouble, just yelp for help!"

104

Pups and the Big Freeze

"Wow! It looks like Adventure Bay froze last night," gasps Rocky, as he, Chase and Rubble race outside to play.

"Whoaaa!" cry the pups, skidding across the icy ground into ...

106

... a huge pile of snow!

"It really did freeze last night," says Chase, giggling at their new snow hats.

Over near the bridge, Mayor Goodway and Chickaletta are sliding around on the ice, too.

"Oh, noooo!" she cries, as her car skates across the icy road and ...

... crashes into a big bank of snow!

"I'm stuck!" says the mayor, trying to reverse out.
"I need to call the PAW Patrol."

"Ryder," says Mayor Goodway over the phone, "the streets are covered in ice and my car slid into a bank of snow. I can't get out."

"Leave it to the pups, Mayor Goodway," Ryder replies. "We're on our way."

Ryder hits the alarm on the PupPad and says, "PAW Patrol to the Lookout!"

Let's roll!

Outside in the snow, Marshall, Rubble and Chase stop playing as their pup tags light up one by one.

"Ryder needs us!" shout the pups, and they head off to the Lookout.

"PAW Patrol, ready for action!" says Chase when they arrive.

"Thanks, pups," says Ryder. "Adventure Bay is super-slippery today. Mayor Goodway slid into a snow bank and she needs our help."

Ryder asks Chase to bring his winch, then tells Rubble to clear the roads.

"Rubble on the double!" says the pup, taking the lead and clearing the way with his digger.

"Great job, Rubble," says Ryder when they arrive. "Chase – it's winch time."

"Chase is on the case!" replies the police pup.

Ryder ties on the winch and Chase starts its motor.

The winch pulls the car out
of the snow.

"Well done, Chase," says Ryder.
"All clear, Mayor Goodway."

"Thank you for rescuing me,
Ryder," says the mayor.

Just then, Ryder's PupPad rings. It's the train driver.

"Branches are blocking the crossing," he says. "And the train's brakes won't work on the icy tracks!"

"We're on it!" says Ryder.

"I know just the pup to lend a paw," says Ryder as he calls husky pup Everest.

"Hello, Ryder. How can I help?" she asks.

"The train crossing is blocked and we have to clear the tracks," explains Ryder. "Come quickly!"

"Ice or snow, I'm ready to go!" says Everest.

She hops into her snowplough and roars along the mountain road towards the train crossing.

"The train driver can't stop," explains Ryder when Everest arrives. "And if he hits the branches, the train will jump the track. We have to work quickly."

Leaping into action, Chase and Ryder use the winch to pull the branches off the track.

"Winch hook!" barks Chase.

Next, Everest uses the trail-clearing arm on her snowplough to lift a huge tree trunk and drag it out of the way of the train.

"Great job, Everest," says Ryder. "Here comes the train. Hurry, Rubble!"

Rubble pushes his shovel along the tracks, scraping the ice and snow away as fast as he can.

When the train approaches the station, Ryder tells Rubble to pull over.

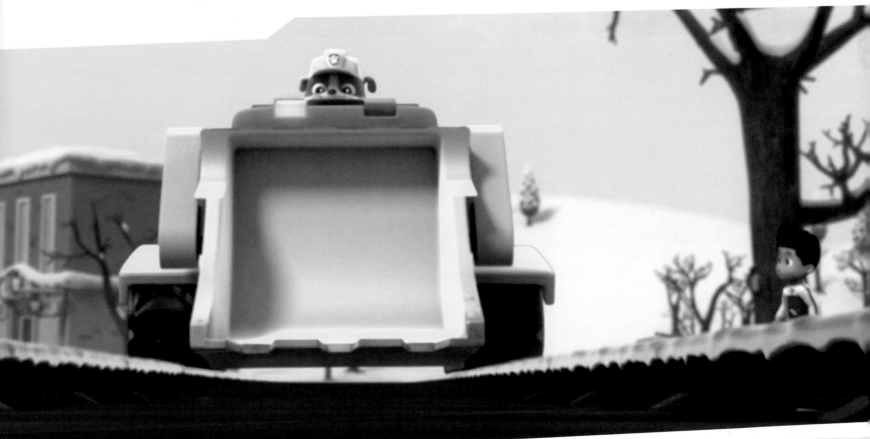

"He should be able to stop now you've cleared the tracks," says Ryder.

"Getting off the track on the double!" replies Rubble.

The train driver puts on the brakes and comes to a stop at the station. *HONK! HONK!*

"Woo-hoo! The brakes are holding," cheers the train driver. "Thanks, Rubble!"

"No problem," Rubble replies.

"We did it!" says Ryder, heading back to the bridge to meet everyone. "Now let's celebrate. Who wants to skate?"

"I was born to slide!" howls Everest, and she and the rest of the pups race off to play.

"This will help you slide, Everest!" cries Marshall. "Water cannon!"

The fire pup shoots a stream of water that instantly freezes into a solid arch in the cold air.

Whoooaaa!

"An ice slide!" says Everest, scrambling to the top.
She zooms down so fast that she bumps into Zuma
and Skye at the bottom.

The pups go flying up, up, up ... and straight into a pile of snow!

"Hee, hee, hee!" everyone laughs, looking at their silly snow hats.

"What a good bunch of pups," says Ryder.

Pups Save the Parade

It's Adventure Bay Day and the pups are getting their vehicles ready for the parade.

"Your pirate-boat float looks great, Zuma!" says Chase. "And Skye, your skywriting helicopter is ..."

"... in pieces! Oh, no. Can you finish putting it together in time for the parade?" asks Chase.

"Nearly finished," says Ryder.

"And then this pup's gonna fly!" says Skye.

Meanwhile, on Main Street, Alex is helping Katie with her pet-bath float.

He ties on so many balloons that they lift the bath up into the air!

"Maybe that was too many," says Alex, as the bath floats away with Cali and Chickaletta inside.

Katie, Alex and Mayor Goodway chase after them, but the bath floats higher and higher until *BUMP*! It gets caught on top of the lemonade stand.

"What should we do?" asks Mayor Goodway.

"I know," says Alex. "Let's call the PAW Patrol!"

Mayor Goodway quickly takes out her phone. "Ryder, we need your help!"

"No job is too big, no pup is too small,"
says Ryder, pushing a button on his PupPad.
"PAW Patrol to the Lookout!"

Marshall, Rocky and Zuma race to the Lookout
as their pup tags light up.

"Katie's float is stuck and Cali and Chickaletta are inside," Ryder tells the pups. "Marshall, I need you to use your ladder to bring them down, and Chase, I need you to keep the area clear."

"I'm fired up!" says Marshall.

"Chase is on the case!" says Chase.

Ryder, Marshall and Chase jump in their trucks and zoom to the rescue.

"PAW Patrol is on a roll!" shouts Ryder.

When they arrive, Chase uses his megaphone and traffic cones to clear the area and make a safe space for the bath to land.

"Everyone, please keep clear!" calls Chase.

Marshall drives his fire engine to the lemonade stand and climbs up his long ladder.

"Cali! Chickaletta!" he calls. "I'm here to get you down safely."

Ruff-ruff rescue!

But as Marshall reaches for Chickaletta, the bath wobbles and Cali jumps on his face.

"Woah! I can't see!" cries Marshall, tumbling into the bath and knocking it free of the stand.

The bath floats off towards the parade of big balloons.

"Woah!" cries Marshall, floating past the balloons.
"It's a big, gigantic ... ME! That's cool!"

As they float away
from the giant balloons,
the bath hits the City Hall
tower with a *THUMP*!
And Chickaletta falls out....

"Net!" shouts Chase from the ground, quickly shooting out a net from his pup pack for Chickaletta to land in.

The chicken bounces off the net straight into Mayor Goodway's arms.

"You're safe!" cries the mayor, happily.

Back up in the air, the bath is still caught on the tower, but it has tipped off balance. Marshall is hanging off the edge with Cali holding on to his tail!

"Hello!" Marshall calls. "I could use some help!"

Ryder pulls out his PupPad. "Skye, I need you to get Marshall and Cali down from the bath float. Hurry!"

"On my way, Ryder," replies Skye. "I've just finished preparing the helicopter."

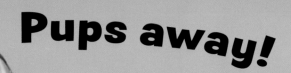

Pups away!

"Let's take to the sky!"
says Skye, heading off
to find Marshall.

"Skye!" calls Marshall,
seeing her approach.
"Boy, am I glad to see you."

Skye dangles a harness in front of Marshall. "Grab on!" she calls out.

"Look, no paws!" says Marshall. The crowd gasps as he leaps off and grabs the harness bar with his teeth.

Skye flies Marshall and Cali away from
the bath and lands them safely on the
ground in the middle of Chase's cones.

"You're safe," says Chase. "And right between my cones!"

"Hooray!" cheers Marshall.

Cali jumps into Katie's arms. "Cali! I'm so glad you're okay," Katie cries.

151

POP!

POP!

Back up in the air, the bath is still floating. Chase runs around firing tennis balls at the balloons.

POP! POP! POP!

As the balloons burst, the bath starts to float slowly back down to the ground.

"Chase ... is ... on ... the ... case," puffs Chase when the bath finally lands.

"Thank you so much, Ryder," says Mayor Goodway.

"And thank you, PAW Patrol!" adds Katie.

"No problem," replies Ryder.

Now everyone is safely on the ground and the floats are ready, the Adventure Bay Day parade can finally begin.

"PAW Patrol – to your floats!" shouts Chase through his megaphone.

Ryder grabs the PupPad. "You're on, Skye!"

"Okay, Ryder. This pup's gotta FLY!" shouts Skye as she zooms along, spreading coloured smoke across the sky.

"WOW!" gasps the Adventure Bay crowd when they see that Skye has drawn the PAW Patrol logo in the sky above the parade. "Hooray for Adventure Bay Day and hooray for the PAW Patrol!"

The End

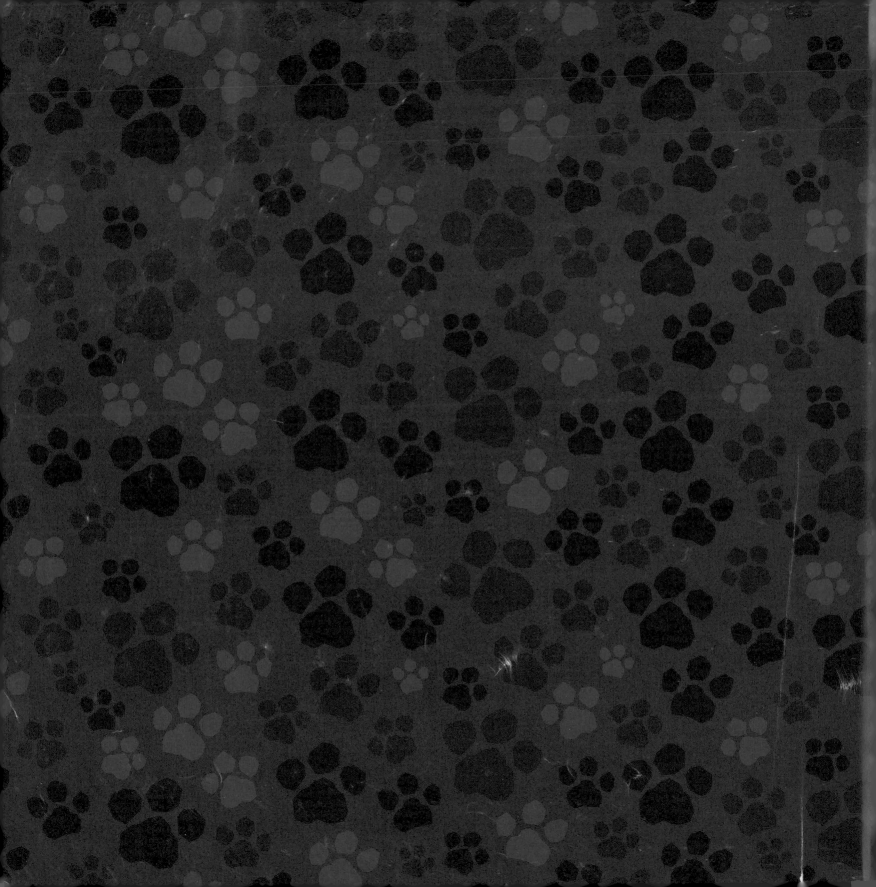